animal planet™

Dolphin Rescue

Catherine Nichols
Illustrated by Bryan Langdo

Silver Dolphin

Silver Dolphin Books
An imprint of Printers Row Publishing Group
A division of Readerlink Distribution Services, LLC
9717 Pacific Heights Blvd, San Diego, CA 92121
www.silverdolphinbooks.com

ISBN: 978-1-64517-684-8
Manufactured, printed, and assembled in Shaoguan, China.
First printing, February 2021. SL/02/21
25 24 23 22 21   1 2 3 4 5

animal planet™

Dolphin Rescue

HELLO!

Dolphins are curious. They often pop out of the water to see what's going on.

A Terrible Mess

Bang! Bang! Bang!

"Yikes!" Atticus spilled the milk he was pouring over his cornflakes. "Who's pounding on the door so early?"

"I'll go and find out," Maddie said. She handed her brother a napkin. Then she hurried to the door.

Mrs. Grady, their next-door neighbor, didn't wait to be invited. She rushed into the Cardozo family's house. "It's a mess!" she cried out. "A complete mess!"

"What's a mess, Mrs. Grady?" asked Mr. Cardozo. Maddie and Atticus's father stepped into the kitchen. He was wearing his bright-orange jacket and rubber boots. Maddie and Atticus knew this meant he was off to his boat. Their father trapped lobsters for a living.

Mrs. Grady placed her hands on her hips. "Someone has dumped trash all over my lawn."

Maddie and Atticus ran to the door to look. Sure enough, Mrs. Grady's lawn was covered with empty milk and juice cartons, egg shells, bottle caps, and paper towels.

"It's my own garbage!" she moaned. "Who would do such a thing?"

"Don't worry, Mrs. Grady. Maddie and

SHORE THING

The area where land meets the ocean is the coast. The towns there are coastal towns. Why do people like to live in coastal towns? Some like to be near the beach. Some have jobs on the ocean, such as fishing. Some work in restaurants, hotels, and shops for tourists who visit the beach.

Marine Fact

OCEAN BOUNTY

When people visit a coastal town, they may enjoy a lobster dinner fresh from the ocean waters.

Atticus will clean up that mess in no time," Mr. Cardozo said.

Atticus opened his mouth to protest. He closed it when he saw his father's face.

"Right away, Dad," Maddie said. She tugged her nine-year-old brother's arm. "Come on, Atticus. Let's hurry so we can get to the aquarium on time."

Maddie was a junior volunteer at the Lymesport Aquarium of Maine. Since joining the team of volunteers on her tenth birthday, she had touched a sea urchin and cleaned out the octopus tank. She had fed a seal and helped paint a wall mural. Today was the launch of the aquarium's latest project: "Save Sea Animals—Keep Our Beaches Clean." Maddie had promised to come in early.

She wanted to help get things ready for the big day. Atticus was tagging along.

Working together, Maddie and Atticus bagged up the trash on Mrs. Grady's lawn.

"Yuck!" Atticus exclaimed, holding some sticky wrappers between two fingers. "Mrs. Grady must have a sweet tooth."

Maddie stopped to wipe the sweat off her damp forehead. Although it was only nine on a Saturday morning, the July day was already hot. "I wonder who made this mess," she said. "This is such a friendly town. I can't picture any of our neighbors doing anything so mean. Can you?"

Atticus shrugged. "You never know. Maybe someone doesn't like Mrs. Grady and is getting revenge." Atticus read a *lot* of mystery stories.

WHO LIVES ON OR NEAR THE BEACH?

Many animals live at the edge of the water. They can find food in the ocean. Rocks, cliffs, and sand provide shelter for animals.

PELICANS come to the coasts in the summer to have their babies. Both parents fish and bring food for the chicks.

SEA TURTLES live in the ocean. They come onto the beach to dig a nest in the sand and lay their eggs. When the babies hatch, they flop down the beach to get to the water.

HERMIT CRABS don't have shells of their own. They climb into shells that other animals have left behind.

SEAGULLS are excellent fliers. They grab scraps of food from fishing boats. They steal fish from other birds. They even grab bits of food thrown into the air by humans.

HORSESHOE CRABS have long tails they use to flip over if they end up on their backs.

RED FOXES dig dens in sand dunes, the mountains of sand at the beach.

The **OSPREY** lives in trees near the coast and eats fish.

"Like who?"

Atticus scrunched his nose as he thought. "Like one of her students, someone she failed." Mrs. Grady taught third grade. Atticus had been in her class the year before, and she had given him a B in Handwriting. Until then Atticus had been a straight A student.

Maddie laughed. "Was it *you*?" she kidded.

"You know it couldn't have been me," he replied seriously. "We were together all morning."

◢ ◢ ◢

Inside the house, Mrs. Grady was sipping tea. She seemed calmer.

"All done," Atticus said. He went to

the sink and scrubbed his hands. "You have sticky garbage," he complained.

Mrs. Grady laughed. "Thank you both," she said. "Did I hear you say you're going to the aquarium?"

Their father glanced at his watch. "I'm afraid I can't take you guys. I'm already late. I need to get to the boat."

"That's okay, Dad," Maddie said.

"We'll take the bus," Atticus added.

Thomas Cardozo was a single parent. He worked long hours and took care of the kids by himself. That didn't leave a lot of time for rides to the aquarium. Maddie and Atticus had a lot of practice getting around without him.

"I can take you to the aquarium if you'd like," Mrs. Grady offered. "I have to go in that direction anyway."

"That's great!" Maddie exclaimed.

"Yes, thank you," said Mr. Cardozo. "That would be a big help."

Just then a crash came from overhead. It was followed by a yelp of pain.

Mrs. Grady jumped. "What was that?"

"That," said Mr. Cardozo, "is my nephew Zach."

"He probably fell out of my top bunk," Atticus said. "Again."

⏚ ⏚ ⏚

CHAPTER 2

Splash!

A tall, skinny teenage boy appeared in the kitchen doorway. He yawned. At his heels was a large, shaggy dog.

"This is Zach Quintos," Mr. Cardozo said to Mrs. Grady. "He's staying with us for the summer." He pointed to the dog slumped at Zach's feet. "And this hairy creature is Norville, Zach's dog. Zach, this is Mrs. Grady, our next-door neighbor."

Zach mumbled his hello. He dumped half a box of cornflakes into his bowl.

"Nice to meet you, Zach," said Mrs. Grady. "I'm taking Maddie and Atticus to the aquarium. Would you care to come along?"

Zach crunched and swallowed a big mouthful of cereal before answering. "No, thanks. I have big plans for today."

"What could possibly be better than a trip to the aquarium?" Maddie asked.

"I'm spending the morning on the beach," Zach said.

"Going swimming?" Atticus asked.

Zach shook his head. "I never learned how. I can dog paddle a little, and that's it."

"How come you never learned?" Maddie asked. Everyone she knew had learned to swim before they could tie their shoes.

Zach shrugged. "I don't know. I guess I just never needed to know how. We don't do a lot of swimming in the city."

"You should take lessons," Maddie said.

"That's a great idea, Maddie," said Mr. Cardozo as he reached down to grab Norville by the collar. He pulled the dog away from the kitchen rug he was chewing. "This dog of yours isn't trained," he told his nephew. "Yesterday he broke the screen door to the backyard. He could use a few obedience lessons."

"Norville?" Zach looked surprised. "He's still young. He'll grow out of it."

After breakfast, Mrs. Grady drove Maddie and Atticus to the aquarium. It was all the way at the other end of the island, about a twenty minute drive.

SEA GLASS

At an aquarium, you can see all kinds of ocean animals and plants. You can learn about the places they live, what they eat, and how they survive.

Scientists at many aquariums study the animals that live in the ocean. They learn as much as they can about ocean animals, so they will know how to help them—in their ocean homes and at the aquarium.

Marine Fact

GO FISH

Aquariums can be large enough to hold a whale shark or small enough for a tiny goldfish.

Looking out the car window, Maddie thought how lucky she was to live where she did. Surrounded by water, the small island could only be reached by a bridge. Everyone who lived there knew and looked out for one another. Maddie sniffed the salty sea air and smiled. They were almost at the aquarium.

A minute later, Mrs. Grady pulled up in front of the bright-white building. Before she drove off, she thanked Maddie and Atticus once more for their help with the trash. "I just hope it doesn't happen again," she said.

⬤ ⬤ ⬤

Inside the aquarium, right by the visitor center, was the mural Maddie had helped paint.

"Can you guess which part I worked on?" she asked her brother.

"Let me see." Atticus pretended to examine the mural. Then he pointed to a pod of dolphins frolicking in the ocean.

"How did you guess?"

"That's all you ever draw, read, or talk about: dolphins, dolphins, dolphins."

"That's because they're fascinating," Maddie said. "Dolphins are mammals, not fish, you know."

"Yes, I *do* know," said Atticus. "You've told me exactly forty-two times now."

A man wearing a bow tie was standing behind the counter at the visitor center. "Maddie, I'm glad you're here!" he exclaimed. "I have something for you." He handed her a small box.

"What is it?" Maddie asked.

Inside the box was a real shark tooth on a shiny silver chain.

"That's a thank-you present for your hard work," Mr. Marshall said. "All our volunteers get one after they have been with us for one year."

"Thank you!" Maddie said. "I'll wear it always." She slipped on the necklace.

"And don't forget Cleanup Day is next week," Mr. Marshall reminded her. "We're hoping to pick up every piece of garbage on the beach."

"We wouldn't miss it for anything," Maddie assured him. "We know how important it is to keep trash away from sea animals."

"More cleaning," Atticus groaned after Mr. Marshall had left. "Didn't we do enough of that this morning?"

"It's for a good cause. You're going!" Maddie told her frowning brother. "Now I have to get to work. The 'Save Sea Animals' exhibit opens in a few hours."

CLEANING CREW

Many coastal towns set aside a special day to clean up beach areas. People pick up all the trash on the shore. They clean up the areas around the rivers and streams that flow into the ocean.

DO TOUCH!

At the touch pool, you can see and even touch some tide-pool animals.

Marine Fact

HANDLE WITH CARE

If you are allowed to pick up an animal, hold it gently in your hands.

Animals that live in tide pools need skills to survive when the tide goes out. Some, such as barnacles, grip tightly to rocks so they aren't washed away. Others, such as sea slugs, hide under seaweed to stay wet until the tide comes back in.

That afternoon, Maddie and Atticus took the bus home. Their cottage was just a few short blocks from the marina where their dad kept his boat. They decided to get off at the marina in case their dad's boat came in early.

Atticus ran ahead when they reached the marina. He liked to see the seagulls looking for fish scraps on the pier. He watched with delight as two seagulls fought for a piece of fish. Then he saw what they were really fighting over. The trash bin at the end of the pier was on its side. Half-eaten sandwiches, chicken bones, and plastic cups were strewn over the wood boards.

"It happened again!" he called to his sister.

Maddie came running. When she reached the spilled trash, she stopped and stared. "Twice in one day," she gasped. "Is that an accident?"

Atticus shook his head. "I doubt it."

"We'd better clean up." Maddie crouched to pick up a cup. "If this stuff gets in the ocean, it will harm the animals."

For once Atticus didn't argue. He got to work helping his sister pick up the trash.

When they finished, Atticus straightened up and pointed to a figure coming toward them. "There's Zach," he said. "He must be coming back from the beach."

Zach waved to them as he got closer, and they waved back. He ambled over to where Maddie and Atticus were standing, a towel around his neck.

"How was the beach?" Maddie asked.

Before Zach could answer, a furry blur raced toward them. Zach, facing the ocean, couldn't see Norville bounding up to him.

Atticus yelled, "Watch out!" But it was too late. Norville was excited to see his owner. He crashed into Zach.

"Whoa!" Zach yelled as he teetered at the edge of the pier. He lost his balance, and with a huge splash, he fell into the water. His head bobbed up once, and then it sank below the surface.

⌄ ⌄ ⌄

A Sea Rescue

Maddie and Atticus stood frozen over the edge of the pier. Norville whimpered softly. Another second ticked away before Maddie sprang into action. "Help!" she yelled. "Help!" But the dock was deserted in the early part of the afternoon. All the boaters were out on the water.

Then Zach's head bobbed up to the surface. He gasped for air. His arms paddled the water.

"What do we do?" Atticus tugged on his sister's arm.

"I'll have to try and save him." She kicked off her sandals and prepared to jump.

"No," Atticus said, pulling her back. "You're not a lifeguard."

Zach sank again.

"We can't let him drown!" Maddie cried.

Atticus didn't respond; he was staring at the water. "Look!" He pointed to a silver shape in the ocean.

A fin appeared. It was swimming toward them. When it got near the pier, it dove. Right before Maddie and Atticus's eyes, Zach popped out of the water.

Maddie shouted, "It's a dolphin! It's helping Zach."

Sure enough, the dolphin was pushing Zach toward the shore. Its broad body pressed against the boy's back as they glided forward.

"What's it doing?" Atticus asked.

"It's pushing Zach to shallow water," Maddie said.

The dolphin stopped before it reached the shore. Zach tumbled back into the water.

"Stand up!" Atticus called out, running to Zach. "The water isn't deep."

Zach scrambled to his feet. He waded the rest of the way to dry land. The dolphin remained nearby, its sleek head bobbing in the water. Once Zach had reached land, the dolphin gave a chirp and swam away.

Maddie waved goodbye. Then she ran down to meet the boys. Zach was now sprawled on the sand. Norville, barking wildly, threw himself on top of Zach and began licking his salty face.

Zach opened his eyes and sat up.

CURIOUS AS A DOLPHIN

Dolphins are very curious about everything, including people. Sometimes dolphins will surround a boat and swim alongside it. The dolphins may leap out of the water all around the boat. Scientists think they might be leaping to get a better look.

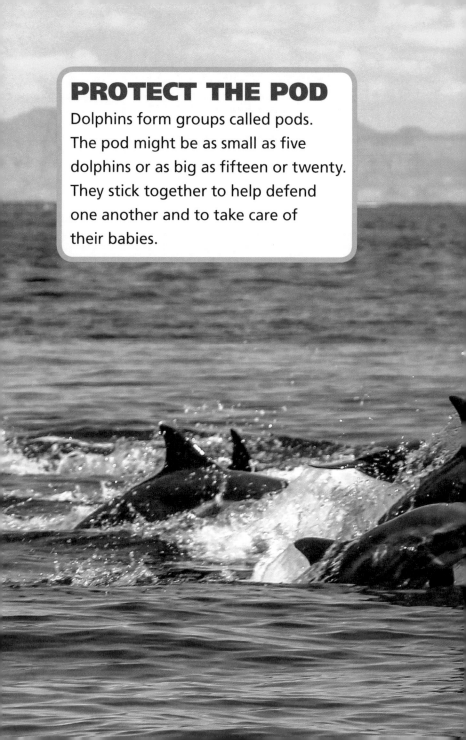

PROTECT THE POD

Dolphins form groups called pods. The pod might be as small as five dolphins or as big as fifteen or twenty. They stick together to help defend one another and to take care of their babies.

Marine Fact

ME TOO!

Gannets fly overhead when dolphin pods circle a school of fish. The birds dive under the water to grab fish before the dolphins eat them all.

Average swimming speed for these dolphins is about 7 miles per hour. They can zoom up to 20 miles per hour for short distances.

Zach spit out some water. He coughed and took a deep breath. "You know," he said, "Uncle Thomas might be right. Norville probably *could* use some training."

⚓ ⚓ ⚓

The Mystery of the Dumped Trash

When their dad got home later that afternoon, Atticus met him at the door.

"Zach fell off the pier and almost drowned," Atticus told his father.

"Then a dolphin came and pushed Zach to shore," Maddie added. "I'm pretty sure it was an Atlantic white-sided dolphin. It was unbelievably cool."

"Wow." Mr. Cardozo shook his head.

"That's amazing! Zach could have been in serious trouble." He looked thoughtful for a moment. "Where is he?"

"He went straight to bed after he dried off," Atticus answered. "He said he was exhausted."

"Well, wake him. We need to take him to the doctor and get him checked out," said Mr. Cardozo. "What were you kids doing at the dock in the first place?"

Maddie and Atticus explained about the spilled trash.

Their father frowned. "Hmm. That's not good. I was telling some of our neighbors about Mrs. Grady's trash problem. They said the same thing had happened to them. Mr. Barone found trash on his lawn on Thursday. And the

Greenbergs on Friday."

"It's a mystery." Atticus's eyes sparkled.

"Yes, one that's stinking up our neighborhood," said his sister.

⩗ ⩗ ⩗

Maddie and Atticus woke early Sunday morning. They decided to let their father sleep in. They made their own breakfast. Maddie got the eggs from the fridge while Atticus went to get the newspaper. He opened the front door. Then he stopped suddenly and called out, "Maddie, you'd better come here!"

His sister hurried over and gasped. Both trash bins were on their sides. Piles of trash spilled out of them and all across the lawn. Maddie spotted yesterday's pizza crusts among the trash. "I can't believe it," she said.

"Believe it," Atticus said. "You're not dreaming." To prove it, he pinched her arm.

"Ouch! Stop that." She stamped her foot. "This is serious. We have to get this mess cleaned up before Dad wakes up."

"Don't touch it yet," Atticus ordered. He ran back inside the house. He returned with their father's camera. He snapped photos of the trash. "This is evidence," he said.

TAKE NOTE

How do you solve a mystery?

1. Observe: To figure out what happened, look for clues.

2. Investigate: Look around for evidence— for example, footprints may tell you whether someone was wearing sneakers, work boots, or had bare feet. Ask people what they saw.

3. Take notes: Write down the details. When did it happen? Who was there? What else was going on?

4. Consider the evidence. Is there more than one possible conclusion? Be logical—consider how likely or unlikely something is.

"You're acting crazy," Maddie said.

"Yesterday I called this a mystery," Atticus said. "I was only joking then, but it *is* a mystery, a real one. Who's doing this? And why?"

Maddie nodded. "You're right. These can't be accidents. Something fishy is going on. We have to figure it out before Saturday."

"Why then?"

"That's the aquarium's big beach Cleanup Day." Maddie straightened the chain of her shark-tooth necklace. "How can we tell people to keep the beaches clean if we can't keep our own street clean?"

"Maybe that's the reason the Trasher is doing this," Atticus said.

"I need to write all this down."

Maddie nodded. "Yes, but first we have to pick up this mess."

⬏ ⬏ ⬏

After the trash was bagged and back in the bins, Maddie and Atticus went inside. Their father was at the stove, frying eggs. "What were you two doing out so early?" he asked.

"The Trasher struck again," Maddie said.

"This time it was *our* trash!" Atticus added, going to wash his hands.

"This is getting serious," Dad said. "Maybe we should call the police."

"The police have more important

SOLVE IT!

If you want to solve a mystery, it helps to have a mystery-solving kit. This should include a notebook, pen or pencil, bags (to carry evidence), and a camera. Binoculars are helpful, too—they help you see things that are far away.

crimes to take care of," Maddie said.

"Besides," Atticus said, "you don't have to worry. Maddie and I are on the case. We'll track down the Trasher."

"I feel better already," said Dad. "Now eat your breakfast. Where's your cousin?"

Atticus shrugged. "Knowing him, probably asleep."

After breakfast, Atticus took a notebook and wrote "Casebook" in big letters on the cover. Inside, he jotted down the names of the people who had had trash spilled on their lawns and the dates when it had happened. He showed his list to Maddie. "Did I get them all?"

Maddie nodded. "Yes, you got all the people. But what about the trash by the dock?"

"Good point!" Atticus scribbled some more. "There. All done. Now what?"

Thursday, July 21
Mr. Barone

Friday, July 22
The Greenbergs

Saturday, July 23
Mrs. Grady
The Dock

Sunday, July 24
US!!!

Maddie got to her feet. "Now let's go interview the neighbors."

Since Mrs. Grady lived next door, they tried her first. But she wasn't home. They decided to try again later. When the Greenbergs also didn't answer, they went to Mr. Barone's house. He was outside, working in his vegetable garden.

He waved to them with his clippers. "Take some tomatoes home!" he called to them. "I have plenty."

"Thanks!" said Maddie.

Atticus took out his casebook.

"We have some questions, Mr. Barone, about the trash that was dumped on your lawn."

"Oh, that." Mr. Barone shrugged. "That's yesterday's news."

"But who do you think did it?" Maddie asked. "Trash was all over our lawn this morning."

"So they hit again." Mr. Barone tugged on a weed. "Don't worry, kids. It's probably some teenagers pulling pranks. They'll get caught before long. In my day we used to TP houses."

" 'TP?' " Atticus said.

"Toilet paper," said Mr. Barone. "We'd throw roll after roll over a house until it was covered in white paper." He shook his head. "It was long, long ago."

He handed a basket of tomatoes to Maddie. "Enjoy!" he said. "And share them with your cousin. He told me this morning that plum tomatoes are his favorite."

"This morning?" Maddie repeated.

"Yes, he passed by about three hours ago. Nice kid."

"That's strange," Atticus said after they thanked Mr. Barone. "Zach doesn't get up before nine. What was he doing walking around so early?"

Maddie looked seriously at her brother. "Get out your list," she said.

Atticus dug out his casebook and flipped it open.

"When did all this start happening?" she asked.

"On Thursday," Atticus replied.

Maddie spoke slowly. "And when did Zach first come here?"

Atticus blinked twice and swallowed. "Wednesday night."

"Exactly," said Maddie.

◢ ◢ ◢

On the Case

"Over here," Maddie whispered to her brother. Crouched behind a large sand dune, she looked through her dad's binoculars. "We can keep an eye on Zach, and he won't see us."

After lunch, Zach had mentioned he was going for a walk. Maddie and Atticus decided to follow him. They wanted to see what their teenage cousin was up to. Maybe they would even catch him dumping trash.

"What's he doing?" Atticus asked. They had followed him for half an hour. After walking to the marina, Zach had wandered down to the beach and strolled along the shore. Then he had ended up at a popular picnic spot that was near a cove only locals knew about.

"He's reading," Maddie said. "Why would he come all the way here just to read?"

"Maybe he's meeting someone," Atticus suggested.

"Yes!" Maddie exclaimed. "What if he has a friend who's helping him?"

"Whoa," Atticus said. "Who does he know who would help him? He's only been here for a few days."

"That's what we have to find out,"

Maddie said. Then she gasped.

"What?" Atticus made a grab for the binoculars. Maddie pushed him away.

"It's not Zach," she said. "It's a pod of dolphins splashing in the cove."

"I want to see!" Atticus demanded.

"Let's go down there for a closer look," Maddie suggested. "No one else is there. We'll have them all to ourselves."

They snuck out from behind the dune and made their way down to the sandy cove. At the water's edge, they stopped and stared. It was amazing. The pod was a small one of five dolphins, including one calf.

"How adorable!" Maddie cried, kneeling at the shore.

Atticus crouched beside her.

SAFE HARBOR

A cove is a sheltered area of water. Usually, it has a narrow entrance and land or rocks almost all the way around. Many kinds of plants and animals live in the shallow water of coves.

LEOPARD SHARKS

are named for the spots on their backs. They are gentle and do not bite people.

SEAHORSE

mothers lay eggs, but seahorse fathers carry them in pouches on their bellies. When the babies hatch, the father pushes them out of the pouch.

SEA ANEMONES

look like flowers, but they're really animals. They wait for fish to swim by, then grab them with their many tentacles (arms).

SEA URCHINS' mouths are underneath their bodies.

The wide, flat bodies of **STINGRAYS** help them glide through the ocean like birds.

OCTOPUSES can change the color of their skin to match their surroundings. This helps them hide.

FLOUNDER lie flat on the bottom of the ocean, waiting for food to swim by. Both their eyes are on the same side of their head.

He pointed to the biggest dolphin. "Is that the dolphin who helped save Zach?" he asked. "That one had a star-shaped scar on its snout, and so does this one."

"I think you're right!" Maddie exclaimed. "And it must be a male dolphin because it's the biggest one in the pod. Look! It's coming over to us."

The big dolphin swam over and chirped at the children.

"He's saying hello," Maddie whispered. "Hi, Star!" She nudged her brother. "Say hello, Atticus."

"I'm not talking to a dolphin. That's silly."

"No, it's not," his sister said. "Dolphins communicate with people all the time."

"If you say so. Nice to see you again, Star."

The dolphin let out a long, cheerful chirp.

"You're right," Atticus said excitedly. "He spoke to me."

The other dolphins swam nearer, although not as close as Star. One of the smaller dolphins touched Star's side and then darted off. The big dolphin gave chase. Soon all the dolphins were enjoying a game of tag.

"This is incredible," Maddie said. "I wish we could join them."

Just then a long, dark shadow loomed over them. Maddie and Atticus whipped around and scrambled to their feet.

When the tide goes out, many kinds of ocean animals dig into the sand or swim to pools of water left between the rocks. These areas make a cove a good home for saltwater animals that don't swim out to sea.

Sea cucumbers are soft and squishy. Shaped like cucumbers, they come in many different colors.

Sea stars don't have faces, but they do have eyes—one at the tip of each arm.

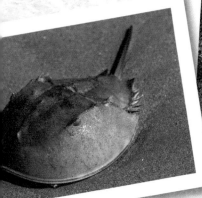

Purple sea urchins have long, sharp spines and tube-like feet that they use to see!

Horseshoe crabs have existed on Earth since before dinosaurs!

Barnacles produce sticky glue they use to attach themselves to rocks.

When ocean waves crash over a tide pool, mussels close their shells tightly.

There stood Zach, a look of total surprise on his face. "What are you two doing all the way out here? Is anything wrong?"

Atticus gulped. "Nothing's wrong."

"We heard this is a good spot to see dolphins." Maddie pointed at the pod, now playing at the far end of the cove. "And it is. See?"

Zach nodded. "Cool. I just signed up for swimming classes at the community center. Uncle Thomas thinks it's a good idea."

Atticus nodded. "You can't always depend on a dolphin being around to save you."

Maddie and Atticus said goodbye to their cousin and hurried away.

"So he wasn't planning on dumping

trash," Maddie said. "He was here for a swimming class."

Atticus stopped suddenly. "That's what he *says*. Let's see if it's true." He ran up the trail to the park's community center.

When Maddie caught up to him, he was reading a flyer for swim classes on the bulletin board. "Classes don't start until tomorrow," he said.

"Yes, but Zach didn't say he was *taking* a class today," Maddie pointed out. "Just that he signed up for them. And here's his name on the sign-up sheet. He probably came and signed the sheet while we were watching the dolphins."

"It still looks fishy to me," Atticus said. "I'm writing this all down." He took out his casebook.

It was late afternoon by the time
Maddie and Atticus reached town. As
they walked past the main square, they
saw their father standing with a group of
neighbors. The men and women had
angry expressions; a few were shouting.

Before Atticus could ask what was going on, Maddie ran over to the group.

"It's an outrage!" Mrs. Greenberg cried. "Something has to be done to stop this!"

"And right away," Mr. Bazzi said. "The stink will keep my customers away." He pointed to a large heap of rotting garbage in front of his flower shop.

"What happened?" Maddie whispered to her father.

"The Trasher has struck again," he replied. "I was out looking for you guys when I heard a loud noise. It sounded like the crash of metal. Sure enough, when I got here I found the trash bin on its side. Trash was on the ground."

"But who did it? Did you see anyone?" Mrs. Greenberg asked.

"No one," Mr. Cardozo said. "The street was empty. Whoever did this must be a fast runner."

The group worked together to clean up the trash. Then they helped Mr. Bazzi wash down the sidewalk to get rid of the smell. Mr. Bazzi gave Maddie a rose to thank her for her help.

The Cardozos headed down Main Street for home. As their father walked ahead, Atticus whispered to his sister, "You know what this means?"

"What?" Maddie sniffed the flower.

"Zach can't be the Trasher. He was at the park when this trash was dumped."

"That's right," Maddie said.

"There's no way he could have done it."

"But you know who *is* a suspect now?" Atticus didn't wait for an answer. "Dad."

⬳ ⬳ ⬳

Dolphins in Trouble

Early the next morning, Maddie and Atticus went back to the cove. They wanted to see if the dolphins had returned. Morning was a good time to go because the beach wasn't crowded. Their father was already out on his boat. So they'd left a note for Zach—who was still asleep—letting him know where they had gone.

As they walked along the shore, nearing the cove, Maddie remarked,

THE TIDES

Tides come in and go out twice a day. This means the water level at the beach gets higher and lower. At high tide, most of the beach may be underwater. At low tide, the beach is bigger. Seaweed, shells, and other treasures from the ocean may be left behind when the tide goes out.

"I can't believe you actually added our own father as a suspect."

"I had to," Atticus insisted. "A good detective can't rule out *anyone*."

"But what motive would Dad have?"

"I can't think of one," Atticus admitted, "but he's been everywhere the Trasher has struck."

"He's our *only* suspect now that we've cleared Zach."

"True," said Atticus. "Maybe we'll find another suspect today."

Maddie scanned the ocean for a glimpse of the dolphins. "I hope we see the dolphin pod again," she said.

Just then a high-pitched whistle made Atticus cover his ears. "What was that?"

Maddie ran closer to the water. "It's a dolphin!" she cried. "See? It's swimming toward the cove." She peered through the binoculars. "I wonder if that's *our* dolphin. It is! It's Star. And I think he sees us."

"Well, he's in a hurry," Atticus said. "He's swimming really fast."

Both children began to run along the shore. Star swam ahead of them, but every so often he would stop and look back. Was he checking that Maddie and Atticus were following?

By the time they reached the cove, Maddie and Atticus were panting and out of breath.

"I can't run another step," Maddie said.

"You don't have to," Atticus told her. "There's the pod. Why are they swimming in circles?"

"That is strange," Maddie said.

Star joined his pod. He made a series of high-pitched clicks and whistles. The other dolphins answered him, clicking and whistling as they swam in circles.

"Is something wrong with them?" Atticus asked. He spotted a few clouds in the sky. "I heard that animals sometimes know when a storm is coming. Do you think that's it?"

"I don't think so," his sister said. "They would just swim out to sea. It looks like they're in trouble. We have to help them."

STORMY WEATHER

Coastal towns sometimes have big storms called hurricanes in the summer or fall. These storms cause big waves that make the ocean waters dangerous. Strong winds and flooding called storm surge can destroy buildings and docks, damage or sink boats, and wash away lobster traps. Tracking hurricanes is important for fishing boats and the people who work on them.

Marine Fact

HURRICANE KATRINA

The biggest storms are given names so that everyone knows which one is being talked about. Katrina, in 2005, caused terrible flooding.

The speed of the winds as they rotate determines a storm's danger. When it hit land, Katrina was a Category 3 hurricane, which means the wind speeds were 111 to 129 miles per hour.

"We can't help a pod of dolphins," Atticus said. "We should go and get an adult."

Maddie nodded. "I guess you're right. Let's go back to the marina and tell Dad. He should be back by now. He'll know what to do."

But as Maddie and Atticus turned to head back, the dolphins' clicks and whistles got faster and louder.

⌄ ⌄ ⌄

All Tangled Up

Maddie stopped walking. "They don't want us to leave," she said. "What if they're in serious trouble? If we go back to get Dad, it may be too late."

"Then we have to find out why they're so upset," Atticus said. He headed off for the water.

"Wait!" Maddie said. "If you're going in, then so am I."

Together they waded into the cold water. They slowly moved closer to the

dolphins. As the children approached, the dolphins slowed their frantic swimming. Several made low clicks.

Maddie and Atticus didn't get too close to the dolphins. They stopped when the water was waist-high. Maddie peered into the binoculars.

"See anything?" Atticus asked.

"Yes." Maddie moved forward a few steps. "The dolphins are circling around the baby. It's on its side in the water."

"Let me see." Atticus took the binoculars from Maddie. "I think I see the problem." He waited until there was a break in the waves, then splashed back to the shore.

"What is it?" Maddie asked, hurrying after him.

CIRCLE OF LIFE

Dolphin mothers usually have one baby, called a calf, at a time. Members of the pod will make a circle around the mother to protect her while she gives birth. When the baby is born, it has to breathe right away. Its mother or another dolphin will help it swim to the surface for air.

"The baby dolphin is caught on something," Atticus said. "I can't see what it is."

"Let's get to the other side of the cove," Maddie suggested. "Maybe we can get a better look from the park."

The two children raced around the cove to the park.

"Look!" Atticus pointed to an overturned trash bin next to a picnic bench. A day's worth of trash—

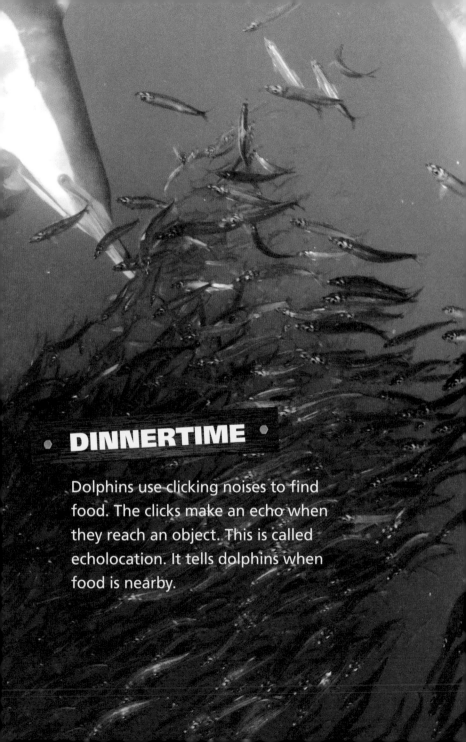

DINNERTIME

Dolphins use clicking noises to find food. The clicks make an echo when they reach an object. This is called echolocation. It tells dolphins when food is nearby.

Marine Fact

BLOWHOLE

The hole on the top of a dolphin's head is called a blowhole. This lets dolphins breathe while their heads or mouths are in the water.

Dolphins are cooperative hunters. This means they work together to hunt for food.

sandwich scraps, soda cans, and fishing lures—spilled out over the ground. The mess went all the way to the shoreline.

"The Trasher!" Maddie cried.

"No time for that now," Atticus said.

"Wait!" Maddie said. "Maybe *this* is the problem." She bent to pick up a thin, clear string tangled in the trash. It ran down to the water's edge. "It's someone's fishing line," she told Atticus.

"So?" Atticus said.

Maddie peered through the binoculars again. "I think the baby dolphin got tangled up in the line," she said. "That's why it can barely move. Somehow we have to find a way to free the baby dolphin." She gulped. "Before it's too late."

Giving Thanks

"We'll need to cut the fishing line," Atticus said.

"With what?" Maddie asked.

"There must be *something* we can use." Atticus started to go through the trash that was strewn around their feet.

Maddie helped him. "What about this?" She held up a metal pop-up tab from a discarded soda can.

Atticus shook his head. "Fishing line is tough to cut. We need something sharp."

MARINE MAMMALS

Dolphins are mammals. So are people. Mammals breathe air using their lungs. Mammal mothers feed their babies milk. Other kinds of mammals also live in the ocean.

The **BLUE WHALE** is the largest animal that has ever lived. A blue whale can be as long as a 737 airplane.

ORCAS are a kind of dolphin. They can eat 500 pounds of food a day. Like other dolphins, they hunt in groups.

SEA LIONS can dive deep to hunt for fish. They can stay underwater for ten to twenty minutes.

Dolphin calves nurse for a few seconds at a time. They do this several times a day.

Some **SEALS** live where the water is cold. They live in large groups—with sometimes up to 1,000 seals!

MANATEES are cousins of elephants. They eat sea grasses and other plants. They are gentle and playful.

WALRUSES have extra-long front teeth called tusks. They use their tusks to pull their bodies out of the water.

"My shark tooth!" Maddie touched the tooth that hung on the chain around her neck. "The edges are sharp. I bet it would work."

"Let's try it." Atticus stood, and they both waded into the water.

The dolphins quieted as Maddie and Atticus approached. Again the dolphins slowed down.

"They know we've come to help," Maddie whispered. She didn't want to startle them.

Atticus gulped. "Now what?"

"We have to get close to the baby dolphin," Maddie said.

The calf was floating on one side. It was barely moving. As the children got closer, they saw that the fishing line was wrapped around one of its fins.

"I wonder if the dolphin thought the fishing line was a toy," Atticus said.

"Just like a human baby," Maddie said. She took the shark tooth and waded closer, murmuring the whole time, "Don't worry. I won't hurt you."

"How are you going to cut the line?" Atticus asked. "It's wrapped so tightly around the fin. You might cut the dolphin."

"I'm not going near the dolphin," Maddie said. "Look—part of the line is twisted around this old buoy in the water."

"That's why the baby isn't moving much," Atticus said. "The fishing line pulls it back when it tries to swim away."

Maddie slid the shark tooth between the buoy and the fishing line and began to saw back and forth. "It's working, I think."

"Keep going—it's almost cut through," Atticus said.

Maddie tugged on the line, and it snapped in two.

"Look!" Atticus shouted. The baby dolphin chirped and dove into the water. When it bobbed back up, the fishing line was off its fin and drifting on the water. Atticus grabbed one end of the line and rolled it into a ball. "I'll throw this away when we get home. That way it can't hurt any more dolphins."

The calf splashed the water with its

• SAY WHAT? •

One way dolphins communicate is by whistling. Every dolphin has its own special way of whistling. Dolphins remember the special whistles of other dolphins they have known for a long time.

fins. It was truly free. Then it swam out of the cove and into the open sea. The rest of the pod followed.

"They probably want to get far away from here after that," Maddie said. "Goodbye, dolphins."

"Don't say goodbye just yet," Atticus said, nodding toward the pod.

Star had turned around and was heading back. He gave each kid a playful nudge. Then he swam away to catch up with the others.

"I think he just thanked us," Atticus said.

"I do, too," said his sister.

⚓ ⚓ ⚓

CHAPTER 9

The Trasher Strikes Again!

Maddie and Atticus waved goodbye to the dolphins until they were silver dots on the horizon.

"Well, we did a good thing," Maddie said. "Let's go home and tell Dad and Zach about it."

"Maybe we'll get our names in the paper!" Atticus's face lit up at the idea.

"Wait!" Maddie held up her hand.

"We're forgetting something."

"What?"

"The trash can. We need to pick up all that trash. We can't leave the park a mess."

Atticus grumbled all the way back to the picnic area. Together the two children picked up the trash.

YUCK!

Garbage on the beach smells bad. And when the tide goes out, it carries the trash with it. This harms ocean water and animals.

CRASH!

Both Maddie and Atticus jumped.

"What was *that*?" Atticus asked.

"It sounded like it was coming from behind those pine trees."

They raced to the scene. By a picnic bench, another trash can lay on its side. More trash was spread all over the ground.

"Oh no!" Atticus cried. "Not again."

"Shhh, not so loud," Maddie whispered. "The Trasher must be nearby."

"You're right," Atticus whispered back. "Now we can catch him for sure."

"I don't know. He—or maybe she—might be dangerous." Maddie gulped. "After all, whoever is doing all this keeps breaking the law—on purpose."

BEACH BUDDIES

Dogs like to run and play on the beach. It's up to you to make sure your dog has a good time and stays safe on the sand.

🐾 Use a leash to keep your dog from running off or bothering other people.

🐾 Bring a plastic bowl and plenty of fresh water, and an umbrella for resting in the shade.

🐾 Bring toys! A tennis ball or other fetch toy will help your pooch have fun in the sun.

Just then they heard a rustling in the shrubs behind them.

"The Trasher!" Atticus shouted, grabbing his sister's arm. "Let's get out of here."

"Where?" Maddie said.

"Anywhere is better than here," Atticus said. "Let's hide out there," he said, pointing to a building.

"Good idea—the community center!"

They took off running. Behind them, they heard thuds and heavy panting.

"Faster!" Maddie cried, but Atticus was already on the porch, doubled over and trying to catch his breath. When he straightened up, he started to laugh.

"Don't stop!" Maddie cried.

Atticus pointed behind her. Maddie
turned, and then she started to
laugh too.

There was Norville, running, and
wagging his long, bushy tail at them.

TRASH TALK

Some animals are scavengers and eat whatever food they can find. Here are some animals that are most likely to get into the trash bin.

RACCOONS can open jars, doors, and trash can lids. They like smelly leftovers like fish and chicken.

RATS will eat almost anything from garbage cans or at the dump.

SKUNKS are smelly pests. They are most active at night and will eat whatever they can find.

FLIES and other insects lay eggs in garbage. When the eggs hatch, rotting scraps provide food for the larvae.

Case Solved

Norville bounded over to Maddie and Atticus. Tangled in his long fur were pieces of deli meat and strands of coleslaw.

"You're a mess," said Maddie, picking some carrot bits off his long ears.

"Looks like our mystery is solved," Atticus said. "Norville is the Trasher."

"Yes, it all makes sense now," Maddie agreed. "The trash problem started on Thursday, the morning after Zach and Norville came to our house."

"And that's why we thought Zach was behind it," Atticus added.

"But the whole time, it was his dog!"

"Norville must have gotten out through the broken screen door," Atticus said. "Smart dog."

"Bad dog!" Maddie said. She turned to Norville and shook her finger at him. "Your days of running wild are over," she said. "Dad will fix the screen door. We'll be putting you on a leash from now on so you can't run away."

Norville raised his shaggy eyebrows as if he understood.

"We'd better go back and pick up the trash," Maddie told her brother.

"This better be the last time," Atticus grumbled.

As they reached the trash bin, Norville ran over. He sniffed for more scraps.

"No," Maddie said firmly. "You're going to be hearing that word a lot more."

Atticus pulled a long rope from the trash. "I can make a leash with this rope," he said.

"Good," Maddie said. "It will be easier to get him home that way."

Atticus made a slipknot and looped the rope over the dog's collar. "There," he said. "No more trash bins for you."

Just then a familiar motorboat raced into the cove and stopped at the dock.

"It's Dad!" Atticus yelled.

"And Zach," Maddie said. "Wait until he finds out what his dog has been up to."

Mr. Cardozo waved at his children.

Marine Fact

SEA LEGS

A well-trained dog can enjoy a boating adventure. Everyone gets a life jacket for a safe day at sea.

GOOD DOG!

Dogs do things that are natural to them. When there's food, they eat it—even if it's in the garbage or on the kitchen counter. They are smart and can learn how to behave. People can train a dog at home, use a dog trainer, or take their pet to special classes to learn how to walk on a leash, sit and stay, and even do tricks.

Everyone in the family can help with training. An open hand helps teach a dog to stay.

"There you are!" he shouted over the roar of the boat's engine. "I was getting worried. Zach told me you left for the cove after breakfast. We thought we'd better come look for you."

"And there's my dog!" Zach cried. He reached out of the boat and stroked Norville. "Where were you all morning?"

"Getting into trouble," Atticus replied.

"We have a *lot* to tell you," Maddie said. "We rescued a baby dolphin . . ."

"And we cracked the Trasher case," Atticus finished.

"And all before noon," their father said. "I'm impressed. Get in the boat and tell us all about it."

The children and Norville piled into the boat.

AHOY!

Coastal waters are perfect places for boating. Whether you want to go fast or slow, have fun or get to work, there's a boat for you.

SPEEDBOAT

FISHING BOAT

ROWBOAT

SAILBOAT

"Where should we begin?" Maddie asked.

"How about at the beginning?" Zach said.

"Okay," Atticus agreed. "It all started on Saturday morning when Mrs. Grady banged on our front door. I spilled the milk I was pouring on my cornflakes and then . . ."

"Oh, brother," Maddie said. "This is going to take *forever*!"

⊿ ⊿ ⊿

GONE FISHING

Oceans, lakes, and ponds are amazing
places to explore, learn, and have fun.

COASTAL CLEANUP DAY

During the last International Coastal Cleanup Day, more than 18 million pounds of trash were removed from coastal areas around the world. That's about the same weight as 800 school buses.

WEIRD FINDS FROM THE 2015 CLEANUP

39 toilets and seats

149 shopping carts

28 refrigerators

Volunteers remove trash, including fishing nets and ropes, from oceans and beaches around the world.

54 bicycles

87 mattresses

97 TVs